Have you ever seen a whale FART ?

A Doogie's Adventures Rhyming Story Book

by Nanette Pattee Francini

illustrated by Devika Joglekar

Have you ever seen a whale fart?
A Doogie's Adventures Rhyming Story Book

To Our Grandson who will always be curious
And to his parents, Coco and Brendan—always curious, always adventurous, always excited to live all of life's experiences.
No words can begin to express the joy you bring us.

Doogie wanted to see if
this whale tale was true

So he ran to the seashore
and his excitement grew

A horse was something
he always dreamed of

Oh to ride a horse
this puppy would love!

Doogie watched and waited
for whales to swim by.

Soon he saw a big water spout
rise into the sky!

But "where are the farts?
I need to know! "

Right then the biggest
whale began to blow

He squinted to see
if he could spot something more

Yet all Doogie could see
were the seagulls soar.

Then suddenly a fine white horse came galloping out

Right next to the big blue whale's water spout!

"Holy Moley!" Doogie
barked with glee

That horse is galloping
right at me!

Who would have expected
a horse from a whale?

Especially one coming
from a blue whale's tail!

I'll ride through the sky
on this whale's gift to me

And we'll happily soar
above the deep blue sea

We'll watch the dolphins
frolicking away

Next I want to ride one of THOSE someday!

We'll fly above islands and
into the sun

Oh we're going to have
SO MUCH fun!

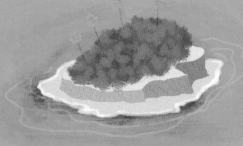

Then to more new adventures
we will go

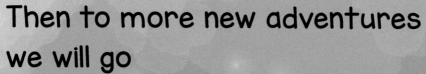

While I give huge thanks
to that whale below

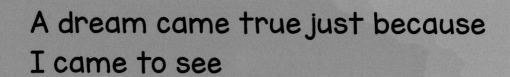

A dream came true just because
I came to see

A whale fart- simply out
of curiosity

More books by Nanette

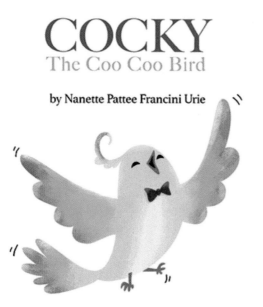

COCKY
The Coo Coo Bird

by Nanette Pattee Francini Urie

illustrated by Devika Joglekar

Doogie's Special
Christmas
A heartwarming story about friendship

by Nanette Pattee Francini

illustrated by Devika Joglekar

Hi! I'm Nanette. After a 30 year plus business career and a lot of "grown-up" writing, I suddenly found myself sitting down to write a rhyming story book in the excitement of hearing that I was (finally!) going to be a grandmother. I never intended to actually publish, but words flew from pen to paper, and after my first book—Cocky The Coo Coo Bird (kindness)—I was off and rhyming!

What began as a series of picture books with underlying value messages for my grandson, has now become my Act IV. And my most fun! A heartfelt thank you to all who made the first in my Doogie's Adventures series—Doogie's Special Christmas (friendship and loyalty)—#1 New Release-Nursery Rhymes (December 2020).

This story book is Doogie's next adventure (curiosity)
His next adventure (courage) is coming soon!

My readers and their little ones inspire me.
Thank you so much for being here.

*A special shoutout to The Highway-Sirius/XM for sparking this idea!

Made in the USA
Coppell, TX
24 May 2021